Elizabeth's Wish

by
Debbi Chocolate

NEATE™ Series — Created by Wade Hudson

Elizabeth's Wish

by
Debbi Chocolate

NEATE™ Series — Created by Wade Hudson

FICTION

Just Us Books, Inc.
East Orange, New Jersey

Published by
Just Us Books, Inc.
356 Glenwood Avenue
East Orange, NJ 07017

Acknowledgments

Every effort has been made to trace the ownership of all copyrighted material and to secure permission to reprint these selections. In the event of any question arising as to the use of any material, the editor and publisher, while expressing regret for any inadvertent error, will be happy to make the necessary correction in future printings.

"I'M SO INTO YOU"
(Brian Alexander Morgan)
© 1992 WARNER-TAMERLANE PUBLISHING CORP., INTERSCOPE PEARL MUSIC, BAM JAMS MUSIC
All rights administered by WARNER-TAMERLANE PUBLISHING CORP.
All Rights Reserved. Used By Permission

"REBIRTH OF SLICK (COOL LIKE DAT)"
(Ishmael Butler, Mary Ann Vieira)
© 1993 WIDE GROOVES MUSIC, GLIRO MUSIC
All rights administered by WARNER-TAMERLANE PUBLISHING CORP.
All Rights Reserved. Used By Permission.

REAL LOVE
Words and Music by Mark C. Rooney, Mark Morales, Nat Robinson and Kirk Robinson
© Copyright 1992 MUSIC CORPORATION OF AMERICA, INC., FIRST PRIORITY MUSIC PUBLISHING and SECOND GENERATION ROONEY TUNES PUBLISHING. All rights controlled and administered by MUSIC CORPORATION OF AMERICA, INC.
ALL RIGHTS RESERVED   INTERNATIONAL COPYRIGHT SECURED   USED BY PERMISSION

IF I EVER FALL IN LOVE
Words and Music by Carl Martin
© Copyright 1992 MUSIC CORPORATION OF AMERICA, INC., GASOLINE ALLEY MUSIC and CAMEO APPEARANCE BY RAMSES MUSIC. All rights controlled and administered by MUSIC CORPORATION OF AMERICA, INC.
ALL RIGHTS RESERVED   INTERNATIONAL COPYRIGHT SECURED   USED BY PERMISSION

For Honey, Pine, M.J.,
and for all the kids of East Garfield Park.

Love,
DC

◆ CHAPTER ONE ◆

*"**R**eal love.*
I'm searching for a real love.
Someone to set my heart free.
Real love. . ."

!zz*!!z#!zz*!!

". . .We be to rap,
What key be to lock
But I'm cool like that.
I'm cool like that.
I'm cool like that.
I'm cool like that.
I'm cool like that.
I'm cool like that.
I'm cool. . ."

!zz*!!z#!zz*!!

Elizabeth Butler was flipping through the stations on her boom box as though the stations were the pages of a rap magazine.

"Hey, cut it out, Liz!" shouted her older sister from the hallway. "Leave it on one station!"

"Elizabeth, if you don't turn that radio down, you better!" chimed in Ms. Butler from the bathroom linen closet. Ms. Butler could absolutely *not* stomach rap music, but Mr. Butler on the other hand, really enjoyed it. He said rap reminded him of jazz: free and spontaneous. Whatever "free and spontaneous" meant, Liz thought her dad was pretty cool—to be a dad.

Liz turned her radio down, but barely a decibel. It was Monday morning in the Butler house and Liz was up doing what she did every morning before school: standing in front of the floor-length mirror in her bedroom, singing and dancing to the sounds blasting from her big boom box. Liz turned the dial from station to station singing every song that caught her ear:

"And if I ever fall in love again,
I will be sure that the lady is my friend . . ."

The melody of Liz's voice blended in harmony with the radio voices floating from her nightstand, mixing rhythm and blues with a little gospel. Music was an important part of Liz Butler's life. She was lead voice in the youth choirs at church and at school. Liz could sing and she knew it, too. Whenever there was a talent show at DuSable Junior High School Liz was in it. Her bedroom mantle was crowded with the trophies she'd won in talent shows at school, where she was a popular eighth grader. There was even a trophy she'd won in a national talent search.

The colorful walls of her bedroom were a living testimony to the rap stars and rap music that Liz Butler practically lived and died for.

Posters of M.C. Lyte, Digable Planets, Arrested Development, and LL Cool J were everywhere you looked. Last month, Liz had styled herself after her favorite star, Mariah Carey. But hanging over the head of her bed this morning was a huge poster of flavor-mad songstress Mary J. Blige. The queen of "Real Love."

This was Liz's last year at DuSable Junior High. She and her best friends, Naimah, Tayesha, Anthony, and Eddie were on the social committee together, and at the beginning of the school year, they'd all helped Naimah to win the school election. They called themselves NEATE. Each letter of the club's name stood for the first initial of each member's first name: N for Naimah, E for Elizabeth, A for Anthony, T for Tayesha and E for Eddie. And as long as they stuck together, the rest of the school year would be a breeze. Maybe.

◆ CHAPTER TWO ◆

Liz smiled at the thought of her friends and began to get dressed for school. She was trying to decide whether to wear jeans or a skirt when she heard humming. Liz glanced up from the mirror long enough to notice her honey-colored older sister. Sandy was busy brushing her teeth, humming, and bumping to the rhythms jamming on the radio.

When Liz looked back at the mirror she realized for the first time how much she and Sandy contrasted with each other in appearance. The mirror showed a thirteen year old, coffee-colored girl whose eyes were of the same hue. She saw a pair of almond-shaped eyes, much like those of the Egyptian queens that she had read about in her African-American history book. She studied her full lips, which suddenly blossomed into a radiant smile. Her shoulder-length braids were neatly interwoven with bright, colorful African beads, which bounced loosely about her neck. The beads always reminded her of Angie, Liz and Sandy's four-year-old sister, who loved to play with beads and braids.

The aroma of coffee and bacon floated upstairs from the Butler kitchen and Liz hurried to finish dressing in time for school. But she took a little extra time to admire herself, and bumped to the easy rhythms floating from her night stand while she finished putting on the final touches. Then all of a sudden a D.J's voice blared from the boom box:

"V93!" the radio voice announced, "is sponsoring its first annual gospel, blues, rhythm, soul, and rap talent search for junior high and high school aged students! Contestants must be students currently enrolled in city-wide schools in order to participate." The radio announcer punctuated the words as though his voice were a bass drum driving through the street in a Fourth of July parade.

"The grand prize to the best individual or group will be a *cool* five thousand dollars. Half will go to the winner or winners, and half will be donated in prizes to the individual's school. Pick up your contest applications at any Rose Records store. The deadline for applications is Saturday, October 10th. We're radio station V93! Your music radio for the nineties and we're looking for this city's next shining star . . . ."

As soon as the radio voice fell silent Liz started screaming at the mirror: "That's me! V93 is looking for me!" she shouted over and over again, jumping on top of Sandy.

"Oh, no!" groaned Sandy narrowly escaping drowning in the current of Liz's waterbed. "Not another talent show," she sighed while making a beeline for the safety of her own bedroom across the hall.

"Elizabeth!" shouted Ms. Butler from the kitchen. It took the sound of her mother's voice to jolt Liz back to reality. Liz hurried with the finishing touches on her flavor-mad outfit. She slipped on the Kente cloth jacket that her parents had bought for her in Ghana the month before. Then she broke out a red, leather baseball cap and a pair of red-rimmed sunglasses. She checked her hair beads and took one last look at her outrageously cute self before grabbing her book bag and running down to breakfast.

Downstairs in the kitchen, she quickly gobbled up her bacon and eggs, much to the disapproval of her mother, and was off like a shot, jogging towards DuSable Junior High. Not only were her feet racing but her mind was racing, too. As she passed the corner bakery images of new clothes, new shoes, a new CD player, and all of the things she could buy with her contest winnings helped to keep her in step. Liz broke into a run. She couldn't wait to spread the good news to her NEATE friends about the cool five thousand dollars in prize money that could be awaiting her and her classmates.

By the end of the school day just about everybody at DuSable had heard about Elizabeth's wish: her soon-to-be bid for the V93 city-wide talent contest. Both teachers and students were behind her, supporting her all the way.

"Go on with your bad self!" Heather Steward and her crowd shouted to Liz during lunch.

"It's show time, girlfriend!" Liz shouted back waving. She was beginning to feel like a celebrity again. She hadn't had that feeling since the last talent contest she'd been in at the beginning of the school year. On the way back in from lunch, Ms. Lewis, the music teacher and choir director, stopped Liz in the hallway.

"Well, young lady," Ms. Lewis smiled. "I understand you're going city-wide with your talent. I just want you to know that I'm behind you one-hundred percent. To tell you the truth," confided Ms. Lewis, "I'd planned on encouraging you to try out, but I'm happy to see you made that decision on your own. Besides which," teased the music teacher, "the choir could sure use some of that prize money to buy new robes." Liz and Ms. Lewis laughed knowingly together. The robes worn by the #1 rated DuSable choir were going on four years old and didn't look half as good as the robes they saw at other schools throughout the city. But Liz wasn't really thinking about choir robes.

"Break a leg, Liz," smiled Ms. Lewis reassuringly. "If there's anybody at all with talent here at DuSable, it's you."

When the final bell of the school day rang that Monday afternoon, Liz made a pit stop at her locker then dashed over to the multi-media arts room. Naimah, Eddie, Tayesha, Anthony, and the other members of the dance and social committee were just about to start the meeting.

"This meeting will now come to order," announced Jillian Wynn. Jillian was the only seventh grader at DuSable to head a student government committee.

"Now," continued Jillian, "as you all know, the dance and social committee will be in charge of all dances, talent shows, carnivals, and other entertainment this year.

"The first dance is in two-and-a-half weeks and we have five-hundred dollars to pay for our music. All of the student government committees have their own budgets, but we have permission to raise our own money if we decide we want to hire better bands or better known dee jays. Are there any questions or comments? Does anybody have any ideas they want to throw out about the bands we should consider?"

Eddie Delaney's hand shot up into the air like a bolt of lightening.

"Eddie?" Jillian acknowledged.

"I know where we can get a *hot* dee jay for only fifty dollars," said Eddie seriously.

"Well, that's the best news I've heard all day," said Jillian looking hopeful and quickly calculating the possibility of saving four-hundred-fifty dollars.

"Who's the dee jay?"

"Me! Crazy Eddie!" Eddie answered playfully. The small group of students giggled.

"C'mon, Eddie. Quit goofing off," pleaded Jillian. "We've got a lot of work to do and only two and a half weeks to do it."

"Well, let's start with the bands first since they will be a lot harder to get," Naimah jumped in.

"Naimah's right," agreed Pete Russell. "Let's start with the bands. I nominate Marky C. He's pretty hot right now—but not *so* hot that he'd turn down five-hundred big ones to play at our school dance."

"Yeah," agreed Kim Chan excitedly. Kim had been on the dance committee last year and was in charge of contacting bands for different school functions. She knew the rates they charged. "Let's not wait until the last minute. Last year we missed out on having Marky C because Chalmers junior high got to him first." Kim looked around the table.

"Yeah. Yeah, let's not go through that again. . .," a chorus of agreement registered from a small inner circle of committee members.

"Whoa! Wait a minute! Hold on," Liz suddenly jumped in. "Marky C plays heavy metal!"

"So what?" countered Pete. "What's wrong with metal?"

"Well, personally, I was thinking more along the lines of nominating a rap group to play at the dance."

"Yeah," acknowledged Eddie and Anthony in unison.

"That *would* be a nice change of pace,"

added Tayesha. "Last year all the committee hired were heavy metal bands."

"What's *wrong* with heavy metal? It's better than that rap stuff," Pete smirked.

Naimah interrupted. "There's nothing *wrong* with heavy metal, Pete," she tried to explain. "All Liz is trying to say is that it would be nice to dance to something different for a change. You know, mix the music up a little. That's all."

Pete sat back in his chair and glared at Naimah. He had lost the race for president of the student council earlier in the year and was still holding a grudge.

"I nominate Kool Moe Gee," Liz offered confidently.

"Are there any more nominations?" Jillian asked.

Eddie's hand shot up again. "Yeah," he said. "I know a band. . ." he began.

"Thanks, Eddie. But no thanks," Jillian cut in. "This meeting is now adjourned. On Friday, after school, we'll take one or two more nominations, if anyone has any. If not, we'll take a standing vote: heavy metal, or rap. . . ."

◆ CHAPTER THREE ◆

"*My* lollipop.
My lemon drop.
Girl, candy must be your name. . ."

"Can you believe what just happened back there?" said Liz turning the sound down on her boom box as the five friends walked home from school. "There's no way we can carry the vote to have a rap band at any of the dances this year. We're outnumbered two to one on the committee. There are only five members who like rap music and ten who are into heavy metal."

"Yeah," agreed Eddie. "The odds are against us."

Liz could hear the gears spinning inside Naimah's head. "Well," sighed Naimah, "I don't see why we can't lobby to get the support of some of the other committee members."

Anthony quickly rejected the idea. "That would be like having the other members come to us, to get us to vote for heavy metal."

"Anthony's got a point," said Tayesha. "There's no way they could get me to change my vote to heavy metal music."

"And there's no way they're going to get me to go to another DuSable dance unless there's rap music to dance to," Liz decided.

"Hey look, guys," offered Naimah, "let's not be hasty. There's got to be some way we can get the rest of the committee to see it from our point of view—or at least get them to compromise." The five friends were nearing their homes on Mary Street. Eddie could hear his stomach growling something fierce. It was almost dinner time.

"Yeah, well, anyway," cracked Eddie, "we don't have to figure this all out right now, do we? At least not before we eat dinner, right?" Liz slapped him playfully across the back of his head.

"I'm with you man," laughed Anthony. "I vote we put this earth-shattering problem on hold at least until *after* we fuel up."

"Peace," smiled Naimah, holding up two fingers in the peace sign.

"Yeah," Liz agreed. "Let's talk about it *later*

'cause I think this is a job for NEATE."

As they turned to walk down Mary Street, Tayesha stopped abruptly and shrieked. "MAN! I just remembered. I'm supposed to meet my dad over at my grandmother's house after school." Without giving it another thought Tayesha turned and jogged back to the corner where Mary Street and Roosevelt Road intersected.

When Tayesha reached the corner Liz shouted, "Yo, Tayesha! Try to make it over to my house by seven, if you can!"

Tayesha turned around and ran backwards, while waving to her friends, "If I can!"

By the time she'd reached the street where her grandmother lived, Tayesha was nearly out of breath. *If I had remembered to go by my grandmother's house in the first place,* she thought, *I wouldn't have had to run an Olympic race.*

Finally, she reached the twelve-foot-high cyclone fence surrounding the basketball court near her grandmother's house. Inside the fence some boys were shooting hoops, when suddenly a loose ball bounced, got away, and crashed against the fence. The boy chasing the ball glanced up.

"Hey!" he yelled to the other boys. "Hey look, man! Look! There goes a lemon drop! *My lollipop. My lemon drop...*" the boy sang teasingly.

"Hey, Lemon. Is your mama white or something?"

Most of the boys in the group shrugged Tayesha off, but two of the boys in the crowd jogged over and began climbing on the fence as though it were a monkey bar.

"Hey, are you an oreo cookie?" one of them yelled. "Cause you look all mixed up to me." All three of them seemed to get a big kick out of that. Two of the boys jumped down off the fence and bent over, cracking up and holding their stomachs while they followed Tayesha along the length of fence. The third boy walked the chain-linked fence with his hands and feet as though it were a window ledge. He managed to keep up with Tayesha even though she had broken into a brisk walk that was nearly a jog. She did not want the boys to see how frightened she was or just how much their words were really upsetting her.

"Yeah, Lemon," the boy walking the fence smirked, *"Girl, candy must be your name...."* The fence-walker leaped down and the three rowdies began laughing again. Tayesha began to run as she reached the end of the court.

"Yo, oreo cookie!" yelled one of the boys pressing his face into the last foot of fencing. He was still laughing. "Oreo. Are you white or black?" Tayesha ran. She ran as fast as she could.

When she reached the front yard of her grandmother's house, her whole body was shaking and her heart was pounding. She saw her father's Buick car parked out front. The last thing she wanted was for her father and grandmother to see her crying. Tayesha stopped to wipe away the tears streaming down her face.

◆ CHAPTER FOUR ◆

By seven o'clock that evening, dinners had been eaten and Liz's house was filled with laughter and friends.

"This meeting is now called to order," announced Naimah.

"Let the games begin," teased Eddie.

"Okay," Liz chimed in. "We already know what we're up against."

"Yeah," said Tayesha. "We're in between a hard rock and heavy metal."

"Well, that's one way of looking at it," said Naimah. "But what we need to do now is to come up with some strategy."

"I agree," said Anthony. "Naimah, you mentioned something this afternoon about lobbying for votes. I'm with you. I think we're taking it for granted that everybody else on the social committee prefers heavy metal over rap. That might not be true."

"You're right," Tayesha jumped in. "Each of us could take two members. Talk to them. See if we can win them over."

"That's a good strategy. But we should have a back-up plan just in case it fails," Naimah suggested.

Eddie stood up. "Didn't Jillian say we had permission to raise money if we wanted to sponsor a better band or a bigger party?"

"Something like that," recalled Liz.

"Then why don't we sell something to raise the money?" Eddie went on. "If we can raise the money ourselves we can hire a rap band on our own. We won't have to rely on lobbying votes from the other members of the committee."

"Oh, no! You're not suggesting another bake sale," groaned Anthony.

"What*ever*, man!" Eddie shot back.

"Wait a minute," Liz suddenly realized. "It doesn't necessarily have to be a bake sale. Listen," she said, her voice trembling with excitement. "My mom and dad arrange business trips for a client who imports fabrics and jewelry from Ghana and Nigeria. I'm almost sure my parents could get him to let us sell some of his items on commission."

"That would be great!" said Tayesha.

"And we wouldn't need any money to get started," added Naimah.

"That's the best part," remarked Anthony.

"Yeah," said Eddie rolling his eyes. "I wish I'd have thought of that."

"Now the question is," said Anthony, "how soon can we get started? The dance is in two-and-a-half weeks. Even if we do raise enough money we'll still need time to hire a band."

"Yeah," Tayesha added. "And suppose we're already too late to get Kool Moe Gee. What if he's been booked?"

"You're both right," Liz coughed. "First," she said clearing her throat, "let me talk to my parents tonight about arranging a commissioned sale through their client. Second, I have to go downtown to V93 radio station tomorrow after school. The primary auditions for the city-wide talent contest happen to be tomorrow. There should be quite a few bands trying out, too," she said excitedly, her eyes beginning to light up.

"I'm getting the picture, now," said Naimah, thinking out loud. "There'll be so many bands trying out that you'll be able to act as a scout and maybe help get us a good band for our dance."

"Right again, girlfriend," Liz answered clearing her throat.

"Not the girlfriend stuff again," Eddie groaned.

"Shut up, Eddie," admonished Liz. "Especially since you've just been elected volunteer tag-along for tomorrow. You can help me scout for bands." Eddie groaned again. "Can anybody else come along?" begged Liz.

"I know I can't," admitted Anthony. "Mr. Shelby is out sick with a cold. He's depending on me to make sure all the other guys get their papers delivered."

"I hate to let you down, Liz," said Tayesha, "but I've got some errands to run after school."

"You can count me in," offered Naimah. "But I'm broke, though. You'll have to pay my way on the 'El' train."

"No problem," Liz winked at Naimah.

"And the same goes for me, too," protested Eddie. "If I'm being recruited, then you gotta pay my way."

"I don't think so," Liz laughed in a raspy voice. "You're cute, but you're not *that* cute."

"How's about by tomorrow I draw up a list of the committee members that have to be lobbied," offered Tayesha. "I'll check off two names for each of us and then stick the lists in your lockers at school."

"Great!" said Naimah. "Okay! Now that we've gotten all that straightened out, let's get out of here. I've got a ton of homework to do. This meeting is now adjourned."

"And I've got papers to get ready for morning delivery," Anthony yawned.

"Yeah," said Liz holding her throat, "and I've got to get home to a pot of hot lemon tea. *I've got a concert to deliver in three weeks.*"

◆ CHAPTER FIVE ◆

The next day after school Liz, Naimah, and Eddie caught the train together and rode downtown to the radio station. It was a long train ride but Liz helped time fly by talking at least five miles a minute. At every other stop Liz sucked the juice from a fresh lemon she'd brought from home to help soothe her scratchy throat. It never occurred to her to just stop talking. Every now and then she looked out of the dirty windows of the Congress 'A' train at the houses and apartments that lined the streets of the West side. Then she'd glance over at Eddie who was reading one of the latest rap magazines.

Eddie was checking out the rappers' latest gear. In his mind, he was busy dressing himself in the funky clothes he saw pictured in the magazine. And then he remembered what had happened that morning. Eddie had gotten up early for school, dressed in a faded flannel shirt, baggy pants, and black scuffed combat boots. When he'd finished dressing, he had turned his radio up, and double checked the mirror to see how cool he looked. He had practiced a quick house move to see if his shoes would stay on when he did anything else besides walk.

"Eddie," Ms. Delaney had called from the kitchen, "it's almost seven-thirty, son. You'd better come down to breakfast before it gets cold." Satisfied with the way he looked, Eddie had snatched his red Chicago Bulls cap off his bed to add the finishing touch.

Mr. Delaney was drinking coffee and skimming the morning paper when Eddie slid into his seat at the breakfast table.

"How's school, son?" he'd asked without looking up.

"It's going great, Dad," Eddie answered excitedly. "I got an 'A' on my math test yesterday and a 'B+' in social studies."

"That is good news, son. Remember what I told you," Mr. Delaney went on, "if you make honor roll I'll get you those Shaquille O'Neal shoes you've been asking for," he said folding the paper and putting it on the table. Eddie was busy scooping a forkful of scrambled eggs into his mouth when he met his father's eyes. Mr. Delaney's eyes didn't stay on Eddie's for long. Instead, Mr. Delaney quickly looked at Eddie's shoulders, torso, and underneath the table at Eddie's baggy pants, scuffed combat boots, and untied boot strings. Eddie sat still with the forkful of eggs stuck in his mouth.

"Son," began his father, "now I know you're not planning to leave this house and go to school dressed like *that*."

"Like what, Dad?" answered Eddie through a mouthful of eggs, his hands thrown up in the air.

"Like what? Eddie, you look like you're ready to rake the leaves. Did you take a good look at yourself in the mirror before you came down to breakfast?"

"Yeah. I did, Dad. I thought I looked pretty cool. All the kids at school dress like this."

"I know, son. That's what you keep telling me. But I'm not the other kids' parents. I'm your parent. And I can't understand for the life of me why you would want to go to school dressed like that. Look at your shirt, Eddie. Your mother just bought you a dozen brand new polo shirts. What would make you want to put on an old faded rag-tag shirt like that?"

"This is the style, Dad," said Eddie jumping

up from the table and pulling on his shirt.

"And look at your shoes. Why are they all scuffed up like that, son?" asked Mr. Delaney pushing his chair back from the breakfast table. "You just bought a brand new pair of boots last week. And can't you tie your shoes?"

"Dad," pleaded Eddie, "the combat boots I bought last week are green. I bought these black boots yesterday to match the black in my shirt."

"Wait a minute, Eddie," Mr. Delaney sighed and took off his bifocals. "Let me get this straight. You just bought those boots yesterday and they're that scuffed up already?"

"No, Dad," Eddie laughed, "You don't understand. I *bought* the boots scuffed up." Eddie sat back down at the table and began stuffing his mouth with toast and bacon. Mr. Delaney put his glasses back on, picked up the newspaper, and called his wife, "Juanita!"

"Yes, dear," said Ms. Delaney swinging through the kitchen door dressed in a business suit and a calico apron. Out of frustration, Howard Delaney put his newspaper down again and removed his glasses.

"Juanita," he began, "you mean to tell me you were with this boy when he bought these boots scuffed up like this?"

"Yes, dear," responded Ms. Delaney. "It's

the style. All the kids are wearing them." By now Mr. Delaney was so upset that if he'd been a steam engine he would have blown his stack. He was fuming.

"Well now, you sound just like him, Juanita," he replied impatiently. "You mean to tell me you all bought this mess at full price?!"

"It's all the rage with the kids, Howard," repeated Ms. Delaney. "Remember back in the Sixties when you were wearing love beads, suede vests, patched blue jeans, and calling it high style, Howard?"

"Well, I never. . ."

"Oh, yes you did."

"Juanita. . ."

"Howard, leave that boy alone. Every generation has something they can call their own. We were young once and we had our own way of doing things. These kids have their own way, too, even though I personally don't see anything at all stylish about wearing rag-a-muffin clothes. But I have to admit those platform shoes you used to wear when I first met you weren't all that stylish either."

Mr. Delaney was embarrassed. And Eddie, pretending to wipe milk from his mouth, was cracking up behind his napkin. The sudden honking of a car horn outside gave Eddie a start.

"That's for me!" Eddie said excitedly, stuffing the last of a cheese Danish into his mouth and grabbing his Bulls cap. "I gotta go, Mom," he'd said giving his mother a quick peck on her cheek. "Dad?" Eddie's voice pleaded as he'd stood in the kitchen doorway hoping the frozen look on his father's face would melt away.

"Go on, son," Mr. Delaney sighed. A tone of resignation entering his voice. "But if you happen to meet any of our neighbors," he yelled at the blur of his son's back, "please, *please* go the other way."

◆ CHAPTER SIX ◆

Eddie smiled at the memory of his dad's face. He thought he would look all-the-way fresh dressed in the gear he saw in the rap magazine. When he felt Liz's eyes on him, he unfolded the magazine and showed her the pictures he'd been looking at. There were several photos of the rap group Arrested Development dressed in a mixed bag of hip-hop gear and Afrocentric grunge. Baggy, neon-colored pants. Dashikis. Brother-man caps and combat boots.

"It's hot!" said Eddie with a dazzling smile as he handed Liz and Naimah the magazine.

"Yeah," said Naimah. "I bought a Brother-man cap for my little brother—his birthday was last week and he really liked it a lot."

"I'm glad you said that," said Eddie taking off his battered Bulls cap. "Because you see this?" he asked pointing to the cap's insignia, "This friends, is old hat."

"What are you talking about, Eddie?" The two girls laughed.

"I'm asking you to go shopping with me after the audition. Naimah, you just said yourself that your little brother liked your taste in caps. And look at you, Liz. If you're not the sharpest dresser at school I don't know who is. Look, all I'm asking for is a favor in return for a favor."

"Well, I don't know, Eddie," teased Liz squeezing her lemon with both hands. "I don't know if there's *anybody* that can really help improve on *your* appearance."

"Yeah, Eddie," Naimah decided to join in on the fun. "That's like a *really* big favor you're asking." Then, once again, the two girls laughed together.

"C'mon," Eddie pleaded. "You owe me, Liz. And so do you, Naimah. So pay up." Finally the two girls stopped giggling and promised to help Eddie shop after Liz's audition.

Eddie's voice was drowned out by the sound of the El train's wheels squealing against the steel tracks.

Every time the train negotiated a curve the three friends leaned involuntarily along with it. By now the train was riding on the tracks high above the city. Down below people hurried about beneath the diminishing autumn sunlight. Eddie, Liz, and Naimah watched as the train passed grocery shops and vacant lots and children playing on broken swings. But it wasn't long before the train sped past the West side and reached the busy hub of the city's downtown.

The three friends were so deeply engrossed in their conversation that when the train pulled into the State Street station they almost missed their stop. Liz began to get really excited as they left the subway stop and headed for the radio station.

Bouquets of flowers decorated the counters at the radio station. The receptionist was sitting behind a marble desk. She gave Liz a number and pointed her toward a crowded room where kids Liz's age and older were nervously pacing the floor, strumming unplugged electric guitars, or quietly singing songs acapella. Liz recognized some of the rap artists from other contests that she'd competed in. There was a local rhythm and blues group called the Children of Soul, with whom she had tied for second place a little over a year ago in a South Side talent competition. A couple of the singers from the group recognized Liz immediately.

"Liz!" one of them shouted. "Hey, look!" There's Liz Butler. As the group of twenty singers swarmed around Liz she reached out to hug each of them warmly and to shake their hands.

"Man! You looking good, girl," said Chubby Blake as he reached out to hug Liz. Chubby was fifteen years old and the lead singer of Children of Soul. They had already recorded professionally as back-up singers with real stars.

"You're looking good yourself, Chubby," said Liz, sparkling with excitement and energy. She was genuinely happy that she'd run into old friends. She'd even forgotten how scratchy her throat felt. Liz greeted all the members of the group and then she introduced them to Naimah and Eddie.

"Man!" said Chubby again. "I just can't get over it, running into you again like this."

"Me either," Liz smiled. "I've been hearing about you. You recorded a record with Tevin Campbell, and you're still speaking to *me*?"

"It's been a lot of fun, Liz," smiled Chubby. "The Children have been offered a record deal. But right now we're just keeping our fingers crossed."

"I'm scared of you," Liz laughed, hugging

Chubby again.

"Well, wait a minute, sister," Chubby exclaimed. "We've been hearing a lot about you, too. What's this about a national contest you won a few months ago?"

"Yup!" said Liz, her eyes sparkling. "The Rawley talent search. Now *that*, was fun."

The two friends went on for at least ten minutes. Suddenly, the number seventy-nine was called.

"That's us!" cried Chubby excitedly. "Children of Soul! Let's go!" He shouted over the excited voices of other contestants.

"Chubby," Liz called out as the group headed into the studio. "Chubby, what song are you guys singing for the audition?"

" 'Optimistic!' " Chubby called back. "By Shades of Blackness!" Then he pointed to the sky and said, "Send us one up, Liz!"

"Break a leg!" Liz shouted back, giving Chubby the thumbs up sign.

It wasn't long after Children of Soul were called that Liz's number came up. Naimah and Eddie weren't allowed to go into the studio with Liz, so they kept their fingers crossed instead. When she finally came back Liz had a great big smile plastered all over her face, which told Eddie and Naimah that all had gone well. On the way out of the radio station, Liz confided that at the very last moment she had changed her mind about the song she had come prepared to sing. She had sung 'I'm So Into You', by Sister's With Voices, and was very happy with the way she'd sounded on the studio tape. "I did it," she said massaging her throat, "but I really had to strain to get it there."

"Listen girlfriend, I *know* you're going to win this contest," squealed Naimah pinching her best friend's cheeks, "sore throat or no sore throat." Liz responded with a slow grin. And then *suddenly*, sunshine spread all over her brown face.

"Yup, girlfriend," Liz grinned. "I believe you're right again," she said with an air of confidence. "I believe I *am* going to win this contest. That, or tie first place with the Children of Soul. Now *there's* some competition."

"Yeah," interrupted Eddie, breaking the two girls up. "That's okay with the girlfriend stuff. Remember me?" he teased.

Pointing her thumb at Eddie, Naimah remarked, "You remember this guy, Liz?"

"Yeah, I remember him vaguely," Liz answered looking Eddie up and down. "He's the Bizmarkie guy, isn't he?"

"Yeah," laughed Naimah pointing Eddie in

the direction of the mall, "looking for some fresh gear!"

◆ CHAPTER SEVEN ◆

As planned, the social committee met the next day after school.

"I'm glad you all made it today," said Jillian Wynn as she glanced around the room. "This meeting is now called to order. Okay, folks," she began. "We only have two weeks left to find a band, get a dee jay, and get our act together for the first dance of the year. So I make a motion that we vote today from the list of bands that aren't already booked."

Liz raised her hand and in a hoarse whisper said, "I know we're getting closer to the day of the dance, but can I make a motion that we postpone our vote a few more days?" She swallowed painfully and tried to finish what she had to say. Her throat had been killing her all day. "I met a few bands at the city-wide talent auditions that I'd like to talk with about being added to our list."

"That's not fair," countered Pete Russell who'd elected himself head cheerleader for the heavy-metal contingency on the social committee. "We've already decided to take a vote. We should take it now while we still have the chance to get somebody decent enough to play at the dance."

"Pete's got a point," agreed Jillian.

"Oh come on," Kimmy Chan jumped in. "What would a few more days hurt? Liz is into music. Who knows? Maybe she'll come up with something hot. A band that everybody likes."

"Yeah. Yeah—" a small murmur rose from the group.

"Okay then," Pete consented, "let's vote on whether we should postpone the band vote."

"All those in favor of postponing the vote to hire a band, say 'aye,' " said Jillian.

"Aye," said the majority of the committee.

"Those opposed," Jillian went on, "say 'nay'."

"Nay," said the members sitting in a tight circle around Pete's chair.

"The 'ayes' have it," said Jillian turning to face Liz. "I just hope you come up with something good, and I hope you didn't just put us in jeopardy of not having a band at all for the first dance. If that happens," she frowned, "all of us will look pretty dumb come Friday after next." Jillian stood up and faced the committee. "This meeting is adjourned until next Wednesday afternoon at three."

"Yo, Jillian!" Anthony called out as the meeting broke up. "Wait up! Tayesha and I want to put a buzz in your ear."

After the meeting, Liz caught up with Le Cao Tho. Le was on the social committee, too, and Liz had been assigned to lobby him for a change-of-heart vote on the issue of heavy metal versus rap. Liz didn't know Le very well. But after listening to him talk for awhile, Liz was surprised to learn that he liked rap music almost as much as she did.

"My big brother got me into rap music," explained Le.

"Your brother?"

"Sure," said Le. "When my brother was a kid in Vietnam, the black soldiers used to walk the streets of Saigon playing cassette tapes of American music. Soul music," he smiled at Liz. "You might say my brother grew up on it. And later, when I was growing up, my brother passed his love for the music down to me."

As they passed the Vietnamese restaurant

on Roosevelt Road Liz asked Le about Vietnam.

"From what I understand my parents tried to escape from Vietnam at the end of the war. But they couldn't get out," Le explained. "For the first six years of my brother's life, my family lived in a refugee camp in South Vietnam. Finally, my family managed to escape by boat to Cambodia. And then, later, to America. When they first came to America," he continued, "they ended up in another refugee camp in Florida. But my brother, Tan, says it wasn't nearly as bad as the ones they'd left behind in Saigon and Cambodia."

Le told Liz all about the concertina-wired Vietnamese refugee camps.

"Tan says the only meals served were rice and, once in a while, a little corn. At the Vietnamese New Year, sometimes scraps of meat were thrown into the bowls.

My brother says there was always lots of fighting because the camps were crowded. But that was a long time ago," Le reflected. "My family didn't bring much from our country. But my brother brought two records that a black G. I. gave to him in Saigon. You ever heard of James Brown?" Le smiled. Then they both laughed out loud together.

"My dad served in Vietnam," Liz whispered.

"But he hardly ever talks about it." Le shrugged his shoulders. As he finished his story Liz looked around at the only neighborhood she'd ever known as home. Growing up in one neighborhood, living in the same house all of her life was something she'd never thought about much. And now she suddenly realized that it was something she'd really taken for granted. Liz was so wrapped up in Le's conversation that it wasn't until they were passing the Polish bakery that she realized she'd walked past Mary Street. When they reached the corner, Liz asked, "Well, where do you live now, Le?"

"Right here," Le answered, stopping to adjust the nylon book bag slung over his narrow shoulder. Le pointed to the huge brick brownstone that stood in the middle of Queen Street. It was a homeless shelter.

"Man!" whispered Liz staring in disbelief at the shelter.

"It's no big deal," said Le studying Liz's reaction.

"No!" Liz coughed. "I mean—" Liz put her school bag down and continued to stare at the shelter. "It's just that—"

"It's *no big deal*," Le repeated. "From what I've heard, it's better than a refugee camp any day."

"No, Le," Liz whispered trying desperately to explain, "what I mean is—I've *been* inside that shelter before."

"Yeah, I know," revealed Le. "I saw you there. But I made sure you didn't see me."

"You saw me?" whispered Liz, baffled.

"Yes, I saw you," said Le. "You were delivering campaign flyers for Naimah Jackson's mother."

"What are you guys campaigning for now?" Pete Russell asked Tayesha sarcastically. They were standing outside the multi-media room where Jillian had promised Tayesha and Anthony that she would at least think about voting for rap music for the first dance. But now, late in the ninth inning, Tayesha was having a rough go of things trying to get inside of Pete Russell's head.

"We're not campaigning for anything, Pete," said Tayesha. "We're just trying to find out if some of the committee members might be interested in hearing some different music for a change at the school dance."

"I don't like rap music," Pete shot back at Tayesha. "And I'm surprised you're siding with

Liz and those other guys."

"What do you mean?" asked Tayesha.

"What I mean," replied Pete, "is who are you with? Us or them?"

"I still don't understand."

Pete sighed and looked around before he answered. "Where do you stand? For the black kids and their rap or with us? What are you?

And at that moment Tayesha realized that she really didn't know.

◆ CHAPTER EIGHT ◆

Liz invited Naimah and Tayesha over for dinner that night. They'd planned to do their homework together and later, mix and match some outfits for Liz to wear to the V93 talent competition. But Liz couldn't get Le and the conversation they'd had earlier that afternoon off her mind. During dinner that evening, Liz must have asked her father a million questions about the Vietnam war.

"So Dad," Liz asked, "were you ever afraid in Vietnam? And why did you go there in the first place?"

"Anybody who wasn't afraid to fight in those jungles must've had something wrong with him," answered Mr. Butler.

"It was a terrible war. No war is *ever* good. But the Vietnam war seemed more terrible than most. And like most of the people who fought in Vietnam, I went because I had no choice."

"My father fought in Vietnam," offered Tayesha.

"So did my dad," added Naimah.

"What about the people of Vietnam, Daddy?" squeaked Liz straining her voice. "The ones who weren't soldiers? The ones who wanted to get out of the country at the end of the war?"

"Well," began Ray Butler, "most of the South Vietnamese wound up in refugee camps at the end of the war. Some of them are *still* trying to get out of Vietnam."

"I know, Daddy," whispered Liz reflectively.

"Just what *do* you know, honey? And why are you all of a sudden asking so many questions about the Vietnam War?"

"Well," sighed Liz. "one of my classmates at school is Vietnamese. He lives in that homeless shelter over on Queen Street."

"You're talking about Le, aren't you?" asked Naimah.

"I know that shelter," Sandy jumped in. "We've started an after school tutoring project over there for elementary school students. It's a shame though," Sandy continued, "because the project's not going to last through the school year."

"Why not?" Naimah sounded interested.

"The building's set to be demolished. The owner's trying to dismantle the program so that she can demolish the building and sell the plot."

"Can't they raise the money to buy the plot from the owner and leave the shelter intact?"

"They've tried that," answered Sandy cutting a slice of sweet potato pie for her little sister, Angie. "But they haven't raised enough money and the building's set to be demolished by the end of the month."

"That's sad," said Ms. Butler.

"Where are all those people going to go?" asked Tayesha.

"Who knows," Sandy answered. "Hopefully, some will find a home in another shelter."

"The rest will probably end up on the street. Homeless again," Naimah speculated.

"It's sad, but it's most likely the way things will turn out," said Mr. Butler rising from the dinner table.

"It would take a miracle to raise the money they need in two weeks," Sandy decided.

"It would take more than a miracle," Liz wheezed, thinking about Le.

"You don't sound any better today than you did yesterday, little girl," Ms. Butler said to Liz as she got up to help her husband clear the dinner table. "I'd better make some lemon tea and rub your neck down with camphorated oil."

Liz frowned at the horrible thought of smelly camphorated oil lingering on her neck and on her night clothes. She was beginning to worry that nothing would help her get her voice back in time for the contest, but for now the camphorated oil would have to wait until after she tried on her snazzy outfits. Liz signaled her two friends by pointing upstairs and placing a finger to her lips. And while her parents busied themselves in the kitchen, she and her girlfriends made their way quickly upstairs to Liz's room.

"Whew!" whispered Liz closing her algebra book. "Now that that's over with let's get down to the real business." While Naimah and Tayesha packed their books inside their school bags, Liz searched her closet for something dazzling enough to wear to the upcoming contest.

"Whoa!" smiled Tayesha when she spotted a green sequined vest in Liz's closet that Liz had flipped past. "That vest is awesome."

"This old thing?" Liz coughed going back to retrieve the piece. She removed it from its hanger and handed it to Tayesha. "Here," she smiled handing it to her friend, "try it on." Tayesha stood in the mirror and tried on the vest. She couldn't decide whether the vest did as much for her as it probably would do for Liz. It fit nicely, but she thought the light reflecting off the emerald green sequin made her skin look yellow.

Behind her in the mirror, smiling attentively, stood her two best friends. Liz with her beautiful, dark glistening skin, African beads, and cornrows, and who was blessed with all the confidence in the world. Naimah, whose skin color, too, was as rich and creamy as a cup of coffee with milk. Naimah knew who she was and exactly where she was going. At that moment Tayesha would've traded all the green sequined vests in the entire world for a tiny clue as to who she really was and where exactly she belonged.

"That looks good on you, Tay," said Naimah studying her friend's face. Naimah was also looking for a clue. Tayesha had really been tripping lately. Liz had noticed it, too. That was the real reason she had invited her friends over. To talk. And to spend some time alone together. But earlier, when Liz and Naimah had tried to talk to Tayesha, she had shrugged them off.

"It sure does look good, girlfriend," Liz agreed shrugging her shoulders at Naimah, as if to say: *You're the smart one. You figure her out.*

Tayesha smiled apprehensively at first. "You think so?" she asked. "You don't think it makes me look—"

"Look what!" Liz whispered jumping to the defense of her friend.

"You don't think it makes me look—pale?"

"Pale?" Naimah and Liz laughed until they saw that Tayesha was serious.

"Look, girlfriend," whispered Liz, "don't make me strain my voice. Green is your color. That vest looks good on you."

"Yeah," said Naimah. "Why don't you let her borrow it, Liz? She could break out in school with it on Monday."

"I'll do even better than that. You can have it, Tay. It's all yours. That is, if you want it."

"You think so?"

"I know so," Liz smiled reassuringly.

After dinner and homework at Liz's, Tayesha ran to the corner drugstore. She walked towards the cashier's counter where a display ad had caught her attention earlier in the week:

Tan—don't burn. Get a Copperskinned tan.

Tayesha picked up the golden-brown plastic bottle and twisted the top off. She squeezed the bottle and poured some of its contents into the palm of her hand. It had a pleasant smell that reminded her of sunshine and of the beach at the lakefront. The woman pictured in the advertising display was blonde and blue-eyed. But her skin color was deep bronze and beautiful. Tayesha rubbed the lotion on her forearm. Her eyes widened as her own skin suddenly turned bronze-colored, too. Just like the lady in the ad.

Tayesha walked to the hair-care aisle and searched. This time she was looking for a home permanent wave that would help turn her naturally straight hair into something with curls or waves—or both. Armed with a permanent wave and a bottle of suntan lotion, Tayesha was determined to show the boys who played basketball by her grandmother's house, and everybody else, just how black she really was.

Without giving it a second thought, Tayesha walked over to the cashier's station to pay for her purchases.

"This is quick tanning solution," remarked the sales clerk narrowing her eyes uncertainly at Tayesha. "You won't need sunlight to tan with this, but you won't be able to swim with it on, either. It'll come off in the water." Tayesha felt a sudden sense of relief. It was exactly what she was looking for. Something she could wash off before she came home from school.

"That's fine," sighed Tayesha. "That's exactly what I want." And on the walk home Tayesha knew that she would finally find a place to be. Not half-here, half-there anymore.

All black.

When she reached home Tayesha ran straight up to the bathroom and began shampooing her hair. She took the home perm bottle out of the paper bag, read the instructions, then twisted the top off the bottle and shampooed the cold wave into her scalp. She let it sit for a moment. Rinsed, and then towel dried her hair. When it was time to remove the towel, Tayesha did so slowly. Keeping her eyes closed until she could muster up the courage to take a look. When she opened her eyes she couldn't believe what she saw standing before her in the mirror. Her hair was not just kinky it was actually frizzy. And it was standing all over her head as though she had just stuck her finger into an electric socket.

Tayesha ran to her room and came back with the bottle of suntan lotion. She opened the bottle, poured some lotion in her hand and smoothed it over her face. Then her neck. Then her shoulders and arms. In minutes she was as golden brown as the woman she had seen in the drugstore advertisement. At first Tayesha smiled. But the smile quickly faded from her face, because suddenly she realized she didn't know what to feel, or how to feel about the new face in the mirror. She had done what she had set out to do. She had changed her hair and the color of her skin. But suddenly it dawned on her that the bronze-colored face in the mirror didn't make her feel as real as the old face did.

◆ CHAPTER NINE ◆

On Monday afternoon when she arrived home from school, Liz opened the door to her bedroom and discovered five huge UPS boxes. Liz tore open the packages and inside she found beautiful African fabric: Kente cloth, Kente strips, kofias, colorful dashikis, and cowry shell bracelets along with other African jewelry. Inside the first box she opened was a note that read:

Dear Elizabeth:
   Your parents told me about your project at school. I hope you and your friends will be happy with the fabric and jewelry I sent you and that your classmates like them well enough to buy them. Much success to you and your new business

venture. I look forward to hearing from you
soon.
    Sincerely,
    Mr. Gilliam

Liz was so happy that the first thing she did was let out a scream. Then when she turned to run out of her bedroom she ran smack dab into her mother.

"Mom!" shrieked Liz. "Isn't this beautiful? Come see," she said dragging her mother by the hand over to her waterbed where mud cloth vests, wax print hats, fabric, clothes, and jewelry lay everywhere floating in slow motion.

"This *is* beautiful," Ms. Butler agreed.

"Let me see, too," said little Angie jumping on top of Liz's bed. Angie picked up a red velvet kofia and put it on her head. She picked up a cowry shell necklace and slipped it down over her head and around her neck.

"See, Liz. See, Mama," she said smiling from ear to ear, Angie jumped down and stood in front of Liz's floor length mirror.

"I see," said Liz laughing at her sister who was wearing everything too big. "You look beautiful, honey-child," said Liz squeezing her little sister's chin. "Oh, Mom," she turned and hugged her mother, "how can I ever repay you and Dad?" she said. "This stuff is absolutely gorgeous! Wait'll Naimah, Tayesha, Anthony, and Eddie see it. I know they're just going to flip."

"Well, now that you've got all of these things," advised Ms. Butler, "the next step should be to get in touch with your friends so you can get started selling. Remember," she warned, "you didn't get any of this for free. You're selling it on commission. Which means you'll need to sell quite a bit in order to make a profit."

"You're right," Liz coughed. She wasted no time in calling Naimah. "Naimah!" she whispered excitedly into the phone. "The cloth and jewelry came today. We need to get NEATE together tonight—at my house. I'd do it myself," she wheezed, "but I'm trying to save my voice."

Later that evening, Liz, Naimah, Tayesha, Eddie, and Anthony met over the huge boxes in Liz's basement. Tayesha and Anthony were busy painting posters to hang around the booth they would set up tomorrow in school. They'd unanimously voted on calling the booth NEATE Imports.

"Tayesha," asked Naimah, did you and Jillian get written permission to set the booth up?"

"Everything is set for NEATE Imports," Tayesha confirmed.

Eddie busied himself trying on dashikis, kofias, and beautifully embroidered strips of Kente cloth around his neck. While Liz searched excitedly through the jewelry, trying on necklaces and bracelets, Naimah sat with a spiral notebook on her lap taking inventory of all the merchandise.

"Hey, look!" said Eddie putting layer upon layers of Kente strips around his thin neck. "This is really cool stuff. You see this design," he said, holding up a sheet of Kente cloth. "This design is called 'gold dust.' My father has a Kente strip just like it. And take a look at this," he said cautiously. "This dress would go real nice with Tayesha's new hair style."

Naimah, Liz, Eddie, and Anthony all looked at Tayesha. They were still trying to get used to her new look. Tayesha looked away. She and Anthony were almost finished putting lettering on the last poster when suddenly Tayesha knocked over a jar of red tempera paint on the tiled floor.

"I'll get something to clean it up," offered Anthony rising to his feet.

"No, I'll get it," said Tayesha her voice impatient and edgy. Tayesha returned from the basement sink with two damp paper towels. She knelt and began to wipe the tile in a frenzy. *Man, what's up with you, Tayesha?* Anthony thought. *All of a sudden you got a new hair do, and you've been acting really whacked out lately, too."*

"Here," offered Anthony stooping down beside her, "let me help."

"I can do it myself," said Tayesha standing up. Anthony backed down and decided against saying anything more. It was already half-past seven and Anthony had a test to study for. "Well, we're all finished here," he said. "No sense in us hanging around. Come on, Tayesha. I'll walk you home."

It was warm outside for an evening in early October. But in spite of that, Tayesha turned the collar up on her peter pan blouse. The street lamps along Mary Street were just beginning to flicker and parents were coming out on their porches, calling their children to come in the house. It had been a long day for Tayesha. She'd felt self-conscious all day long about the green sequined vest, her "tan," and her new hair style.

"Oh, Tayesha!" Kimmy had said excitedly when she first saw her in morning gym class. "You really look cute with your hair like that. And what have you done to your skin? Did you go to a tanning salon? That looks really cool."

But some of the other kids in her other classes hadn't thought so. Sheila Jackman had asked her in front of the whole English class what had happened to her hair. And then she asked Tayesha what was it that she had on her skin? Tayesha had spent the remainder of the school day trying to avoid Naiamah, Liz, Eddie, and Anthony.

"Tayesha!" Her mother had practically blown a gasket at breakfast that morning. "What have you done to your hair?" said Ms. Williams almost speechless. "It looks like you've gone and cut it."

"I didn't cut it, Mom," Tayesha tried to defend herself. "I just permed it. A little. "

"A little?" said Ms. Williams.

"I wanted to wear an Afro," Tayesha lied, "like Daddy did, back in the Sixties.

"An Afro?" laughed Mr. Williams good naturedly, nursing his first hot cup of coffee of the day. "Why it's been years since I've seen an Afro." His reflective expression quickly changed back into a smile as he looked his daughter over. "She looks cute, though, doesn't she, hon?" Mr. Williams finally decided.

Ms. Williams ignored her husband's comments and in a serious tone ordered, "No more permanents without permission. Do you understand me?" she scolded Tayesha.

"Yes M'am," Tayesha promised, rising from

the breakfast table in such a hurry that she knocked over a glass of milk. She had been in more of a hurry to get out of the house than she had been to get to school. After school, Tayesha had scrubbed the tanning lotion from her face before returning to Mary Street.

At dinner time, Tayesha couldn't eat anything. She'd sat at the dinner table pushing her food around the plate of china with her fork. She studied her mother and father's faces and realized for the first time that although she had her father's eyes and her mother's complexion, she didn't see herself completely in either of them.

"Aren't you hungry?" her mother had asked. But Tayesha hadn't felt like talking. Her mother had touched her face and said it felt very hot. Then her father had taken her upstairs and put her to bed, and, oddly enough, Tayesha didn't mind at all. She didn't know if she was ill or not, but she felt so bad she was quite glad to be made a fuss of. Not that it improved the situation, but it was some comfort. Later, it was all she could do to convince her parents that she felt better. Good enough to walk a couple of houses down the street to Liz's house.

By nightfall, Tayesha was glad the day had come and gone. Walking beside Anthony now in the shadow of dusk, the maples and elms that dotted the sidewalks of Mary Street looked like soldiers in silhouette to her. But even under the cover of dusk, Anthony could see that something was up with Tayesha.

"Tayesha," Anthony finally spoke. "Can I ask you something?"

Tayesha felt uneasy. "About what?" she said defensively.

"Well," began Anthony cautiously. "It's about your hair."

"What about my hair? It's just permed that's all."

"Oh, there's nothing wrong with your hair." Anthony said quietly. "I mean it looks nice and everything," he paused. "I was just trying to figure out *why* you'd changed it." Then he added quickly, "What I mean is, it looked nice *before* you changed it."

"It's just something new I'm trying out," Tayesha lied.

"But why?" Anthony pressed. "And why did you have that make-up on in school today?"

"That wasn't make-up," Tayesha sounded defensive. Her feelings were hurt. "I thought you were my friend," she said now close to tears. "You just don't understand, Anthony. You don't even know what's going on."

"That's why I'm asking you, Tayesha. Because I *am* your friend," Anthony answered. For a moment they both walked in silence. "If I weren't your friend I wouldn't be here. What's up, Tayesha?" Anthony asked again. "What's going on? This thing about your color isn't bothering you, is it?"

Together the two friends crossed the Williams' lawn and sat down on Tayesha's front porch steps. Between sobs, Tayesha told Anthony about the three boys at the basketball court.

About how they'd teased her and called her "oreo cookie." She described the nasty remarks Pete Russell had made following the last social committee meeting.

"You shouldn't worry about what other people say," Anthony tried to console her. "Those guys don't know anything about you, Tayesha. Your skin color doesn't tell them who Tayesha is. Just because your skin is lighter doesn't make those guys at the basketball court any blacker than you. There's no right or wrong way to be black. Just be you. And as far as Pete Russell is concerned, he's hopeless if he thinks that only black people listen to rap music. " Anthony was quiet for a moment. "You know what you gotta do?" he went on.

"What?" asked Tayesha wiping the tears from her eyes.

"The next time you go past that basketball court and you see those guys? You WALK! Don't run. And you tell those jerks that your name ain't oreo. Tell them you're as black as they are—and more intelligent, too. At least you know that black people come in all colors. And keep on stepping."

Anthony took his glasses off and Tayesha looked at his face. It was nearly dark, but by the light of the moon she noticed for the first time how kind his eyes were.

"I have to go," said Anthony, putting on his glasses. "Mr. Shelby's still out sick and I have to make sure the other boys deliver their papers in the morning." As he turned to cross the lawn Tayesha called out to him. He stopped and looked back. "But you remember what I told you, you understand, Tayesha?"

Tayesha nodded and tried to smile.

"Just be yourself, Tayesha. Just be *you*."

◆ CHAPTER TEN ◆

The next day, Liz limped in sheer agony towards the NEATE Imports booth that Tayesha and Anthony had set up near the school cafeteria. When she finally reached the booth she grabbed the nearest chair and slowly eased herself down into it. Then she carefully counted out fifty, one dollar bills from the NEATE treasury, money they would use to make change for their sales. All the while she counted, Liz squinted at the pain throbbing in her ankle.

When Eddie and Naimah showed up, Eddie took one look at Liz's swollen ankle and whistled. "Man! What happened to you?"

"What does it look like?" Liz snapped at Eddie out of frustration. But it didn't come out right. Liz's voice had deteriorated from yesterday. Today, it was less than a squeak. No sooner had she gone mad dog on Eddie then she immediately felt bad for having taken her frustration out on a friend.

"I fell down the stairs in the girls' locker room this morning," Liz explained half apologetically.

"That looks pretty swollen," Naimah offered her sympathies.

"Yeah," said Eddie. "It looks like your chances of making that contest are getting dimmer and dimmer."

Liz wore a hurtful look on her face. *Why did you have to say something stupid like that, Eddie?* she thought to herself. But Eddie had hit the nail right on the head. Lately Liz's fear of not making it to the talent show had begun to mushroom. How could she compete when she had laryngitis? And she wouldn't be able to dance with a sprained ankle, either.

Kids were lining up at the cafeteria door waiting for the bell to ring. Liz decided to concentrate on the booth. If sales from the booth turned out to be a success today, maybe it would give her spirits a much needed boost. The very first item Liz sold was a wax print hat to Ms. Lewis, the chorus teacher. Naimah sold a couple of inexpensive cowry shell bracelets to two of her classmates. Eddie was supposed to be helping

Liz and Naimah run the booth, too. But all he seemed to be interested in was selling himself.

"Hey, gorgeous," Eddie yelled over the noise of the lunch crowd to Camilla Younger. "Have I got a beautiful head wrap to go with that pretty face or what?" Camilla was a seventh grader but she was small for her age and could easily have passed for a fifth or sixth grader.

"Hi, Eddie." Camilla smiled, and tore herself away from the crowd. Eddie stood up and held a multi-colored cloth in front of him.

"Have you ever seen anything so beautiful?" he asked. Camilla ran her hand along the lavender and periwinkle floral design. She especially liked the design of the macaw bird printed in the center of the cloth. The colors were brilliant.

"It is beautiful," Camilla said admiringly. "But I can't afford this."

"Can't afford it?" laughed Eddie. "How can you not afford it? Camilla," said Eddie in his best imitation of a used car salesman, "this is a real live continental import. This stuff wasn't made in Hoboken, New Jersey, and stamped Ghana on the docks. This head wrap was handsewn by brothers and sisters living in Africa. "Camilla," implored Eddie, "Camilla, read my lips. This head wrap is the real McCoy," Eddie smiled at the cute underclassman.

"I know it's real," laughed Camilla. "That's why I said I couldn't afford it, Eddie."

While Eddie flirted, Liz and Naimah tried to sell items to teachers and staff passing through the cafeteria. In between sales Liz kept an eye on Eddie. Every now and then she nudged Naimah with an elbow to remind her to keep an eye on "Fast" Eddie, too.

"Listen, Camilla," Eddie confided. "We're not talking lunch money, here. We're talking allowance. We're talking time. Ever heard of buying on time, Camilla?" Eddie whispered in her ear.

"It would take *three weeks* of allowance to buy that head wrap!" protested Camilla.

"One *short* week," Eddie corrected, "on Eddie's easy installment plan. Camilla," he said stepping back, holding up the head wrap again, "this isn't just an African print. This is a work of art." He winked at Camilla and smiled. "Tell you what," said Eddie catching the young customer off guard, "why don't we talk about it over lunch? My treat." Camilla smiled shyly as Eddie folded the print and placed it back on the shelf.

"Uh, excuse me, Eddie!" Liz croaked over the noisy crowd gathering around the booth. She got up and limped over to where he stood. "Could I talk with you for a minute?" Adding to Liz's frustration was that she was having to strain her voice when she should've been trying to save it for the talent competition. Eddie excused himself, and while an admiring Camilla waited for him at the cafeteria entrance, he and Liz engaged in a shouting match sort of—Liz's "shout" was more like a whisper.

"Excuse *me*, Eddie," Liz began, "but we're not selling anything on 'time.' We barely have enough time to get things sold and return the money for our commission. The dance is in two weeks," she reminded him.

"I know," Eddie said defensively. "I've got everything under control. The girl wants to buy a head wrap and I'm trying to help her, that's all."

"Look, Eddie," Liz's voice was getting more and more hoarse, "we need you here in the booth," she said wincing at the pain in her ankle. "That was the agreement. Everybody's supposed to work during their lunch and study hours."

"I'm coming back," whined Eddie. He glanced down at Liz's foot. "You're just upset because you've lost your voice and you sprained your ankle. And now you're mad at the whole world because you might not make it to the talent contest." *Leave it to Eddie to drive it all home again,* thought Liz.

"Just do what you promised, Eddie that's all," Liz finally finished. "We've got a lot to do between now and the dance, and we're going to need all the money and all the help we can get." Her voice was gone.

Liz waved to Naimah who was running the NEATE booth alone. She rolled her eyes at Eddie and then she limped back to the booth to give Naimah a hand.

By the time the cafeteria crowd thinned out it was time for Anthony and Tayesha to run the booth. Only half the day was gone but already Liz was exhausted, and her throat ached.

"Girlfriend, you don't look so good," said Naimah to her best friend.

"And I don't sound so good, either," whispered Liz squeezing her throat. "And you know something else," she confessed, "Eddie's right. I'm seriously thinking about dropping out of the talent contest."

Naimah put her arm around Liz's shoulder. "Now you listen up, girlfriend," she began, "you're just tired, your throat's a little sore, and your ankle hurts. But still, those sound like pretty poor excuses for dropping out of the competition. Remember, *you* were the one who said this competition meant more than just putting another feather in your cap. What about the prizes the school could benefit from? What about the new gowns for the school choir you've been wishing for over the past two years? What ever happened to all of that? Or was it just talk, Liz?" Naimah paused for a moment. "And there's something else I've been meaning to talk with you about, girlfriend. Did you ever stop to think about how far your prize money would go if you were to donate it to the Queen Street homeless shelter?"

"WHAT! Liz's voice let out a hoarse scream. "Don't even try it, Naimah," her voice squeaked. "You're really out of bounds this time!"

"Just hold on a minute," Naimah insisted. "Listen up, girlfriend. How many more leather jumpsuits and CD players do you really need?"

"You're nuts. You know that?" answered Liz. "If I *do* win, Naimah, the prize money is all mine, to do with whatever I please," she coughed massaging her throat with both hands.

"All I'm saying," conceded Naimah, "is that it would be a nice gesture."

"It would be more than that," whispered Liz. "It would be a minor miracle." Both girls looked at each other and then laughed.

"Listen, girlfriend," Naimah suggested,

"why don't you stop by the nurse's office. Get off that ankle, and stop talking so much," she smiled.

"Can't," Liz answered in a raspy voice. "Geometry test next period.

"Well, at least promise me you'll go straight home from school this afternoon and give that soulful voice of yours a rest. Get it pumped up for the contest."

"Promise," whispered Liz smiling.

"And promise you'll at least *think* about the Queen Street shelter thing."

"That's a huge favor," Liz conceded, "but I'll *think* about it."

Before she left for class Liz counted the money in the metal cash box. They'd started out with fifty dollars to make change. So far they'd only made twenty-five dollars profit. Sure, there had been a big lunch-hour crowd, but not a lot of buying and selling had taken place. Twenty-five dollars wasn't enough to hire a rock *or* a rap group. Not to mention a decent enough band to play at the first DuSable Junior High School dance of the year.

◆ CHAPTER ELEVEN ◆

On Wednesday Liz, Naimah, Tayesha, Eddie, and Anthony held their own meeting before the social committee gathered to cast votes on the band for the first school dance. Liz and her friends wanted to compare notes on whom they had gotten to vote for rap music, because they weren't selling enough items from their import booth to come up with the money to hire a rap band. And to make matters worse, Eddie had almost depleted the store by selling *more* than just a few items on "time." Which meant that the merchandise Eddie had "sold" had to be taken off of the display shelves.

"So how did you guys do? Did anybody get any votes for rap music?" Naimah asked.

"Well," whispered Liz, "I was able to pull at least *one* vote away from the heavy-metal contingency. But I can't take full credit for it."

"You did better than I did," admitted Naimah. "I spent two lunch hours trying to persuade Adam Young and Dean Walters to stop giving the music a bad rap. I didn't have any luck at all."

"Yeah," Anthony agreed. "Tayesha and I tried teaming up on Kimmy, Jillian, and Sikander. But they weren't having it."

"Jillian did at least agree to sleep on it," Tayesha acknowledged.

"And that butthead Pete Russell. Man!" whistled Anthony under his breath. "He tried to give Tayesha a hard way to go."

A chill went up Tayesha's spine. "Ooo," she shivered, "please, don't even mention that narrow-minded creep."

"Who'd *you* get to vote for rap music, Liz?" asked Naimah.

"Le Cao Tho," answered Liz. "Seems his brother grew up listening to R & B in Vietnam, and passed his love for soul music down to Le." While Naimah took a tally of votes in a spiral notebook, Liz's mind drifted back to the afternoon she and Le had walked home together from school.

Liz remembered Le's story of his brother's first encounter with soul music in Vietnam, and how Le had grown up listening to James Brown's music. She remembered how she'd felt when she found out that Le lived in a homeless shelter right around the corner from where she lived. Suddenly, Naimah's voice interrupted Liz's day dreams.

"That makes six votes for rap and nine votes for heavy metal," calculated Naimah.

After Liz had read from the list of bands she'd collected at the city-wide auditions, Jillian called for a vote. They debated for ten minutes before finally narrowing it down to the two groups originally chosen: Kool Moe Gee and Marky C.

"Okay," groaned Jillian, "let's get this over with. All those in favor of hiring Kool Moe Gee for the first dance raise your hands." Liz, Naimah, Tayesha, Anthony, Eddie, and Le raised their hands. To everyone's surprise Jillian raised her hand, too. "Okay," Jillian counted. "That's seven for Kool Moe Gee." Altogether there were fifteen members present in the room. Jillian opened a spiral note pad and recorded the number voting in her book. "Okay," she went on. "All those in favor of hiring Marky C for the first dance raise your hands."

All of a sudden a smirk spread over Pete Russell's face like a dark cloud in the sky. By the time the storm had cleared, there were eight frantic hands waving nervously in the air.

"The 'ayes' have it," Jillian conceded. And then she quickly began to delegate responsibility for the details of the dance to subcommittees.

"Kimmy," she said in a serious tone, "you'll be responsible for contacting the band to see if they're available for our dance date."

"Pete," she half ordered, "you'll be in charge of clean-up after the dance." At that moment, Pete had a look on his face that might've made anyone think he'd just bought the Brooklyn Bridge for a penny.

"Bet!" he answered giving Jillian the thumbs up sign.

"Tayesha and Anthony," continued Jillian, "you two will be responsible for refreshments."

"Sure," the two friends smiled in unison.

"And the rest of you guys will be expected to pitch in when you are needed. Oh, and Liz," Jillian added, "since you're the creative one around here, you'll be in charge of decorating the gym and getting the sound system set up. See Ed and Dean for money to buy streamers and balloons."

"Look at me!" protested Liz in a hoarse

whisper. "I'm practically on crutches. How am I supposed to go about getting the gym decorated?"

"Sorry," offered Jillian sympathetically. "You'll have to get somebody to help you, Liz. We really need you."

Great! Liz thought to herself. *Not only are they going to bombard the place with nothing but heavy metal music, now I'm responsible for decorating a gym for a dance that I probably won't even be going to.*

After the meeting, Liz sulked and limped all the way down Roosevelt Road. When she reached Pulaski, she thought she heard someone calling her.

"Elizabeth! Elizabeth! Wait up!" It didn't take Liz long to recognize Le. He was running down the street behind her. When he reached the intersection he stopped at the traffic light, but he was still out of breath by the time he crossed the street where Liz was waiting.

"What happened to you?" he asked, breathing heavily, looking down at Liz's ankle.

"Sprained it in gym," Liz answered as they continued walking. The swelling had gone down some, but walking on it was still just as painful as it had been yesterday.

"That's too bad," said Le. "What about the

competition you're supposed to be in?"

"Right now it doesn't look too good," Liz answered somberly.

"I'm sorry," said Le. "I wanted to apologize," he said, still a little winded.

"For what?" Liz laughed a little, "it's not your fault."

"I'm sorry the social committee vote didn't go your way."

"Oh that," said Liz.

"I know how much it meant to you," Le said.

"Thanks," Liz whispered sincerely. "But we didn't do too badly. After all, we came within one vote. Maybe next time," she said hopefully. "Anyway, I'm glad you caught up with me. I meant to thank you, too, for throwing your vote our way."

As they walked, the two friends talked about music, school, and the upcoming talent competition. When they reached the corner store, Liz stopped abruptly and knocked playfully on her head as though it were a wooden door.

"The lights are on," she joked, "but nobody's at home." She paused. "Tell me something, Le. Why is it that everytime I walk home from school with you I walk right pass the street I live on?"

"I don't know," Le smiled, shrugging his narrow shoulders. "Maybe today it means it's time you met my brother." And then, without warning, Le grabbed Liz's hand and led her across Queen Street to the homeless shelter where he lived with his family.

It was approaching late afternoon at the shelter. Liz and Le walked into an open room where earlier that morning, before school had begun, Le had slept with other children on thin, worn mattresses. But now, in the vague stillness of the autumn afternoon, women hovered around a black-and-white television set while their kids ran about wildly.

A boy poured milk all over himself as he tried unsuccessfully to drink it. His mother was resting on the couch, taking no notice of him. Liz had thought there would at least be beds or cots in the shelter. She wore a look on her face that hid the shock of what she saw. She and Le walked from room to room, each room seemingly having fewer mattresses and more children than the one before, until they finally caught up with Tan, Le's older brother. Tan was a short, thin young man in his late twenties. He wore a faded Bulls t-shirt, a pair of green army fatigue pants, and brown leather shoes. When Le introduced them, Tan reached for Liz's hand and shook it vigorously.

"Soul sister—" Le's brother began.

◆ CHAPTER TWELVE ◆

"Testing, testing. One, two, three. Testing, testing. One, two, three." Finally, after drinking what had seemed to her to be gallons of her mother's hot lemon tea, Liz's voice was making a comeback. But her ankle was still stiff and sore. Liz tapped lightly on the microphones that she, Eddie, Anthony, Tayesha, and Naimah had just set up for a trial run in the gymnasium for next week's dance. To help test the school's sound system, Eddie had brought along some of his own stereo equipment, some cassettes, and a few CDs, too.

"Hey, girlfriend," Eddie teased Liz, "your voice has finally come back. Gee whiz!"

"That's right, Money," Liz joked grabbing the microphone. "Want me to sing something soulful for you?"

Eddie covered his ears with both hands. "I thought we were friends," he laughed.

"You're missing a few speaker wires here, man," interrupted Anthony.

"Yeah, I know," acknowledged Eddie. "I usually just rig my system up at home. You know—a few co-axle cables here, a few speaker wires there."

"You're going to need some extra co-axle cables to test the school's system with your box," explained Anthony. "Otherwise you're not going to get anything but static."

"Let's look around backstage to see if we can find something to rig it up with," suggested Liz. She hobbled backstage with her friends and searched through cartons and boxes of lighting equipment. They found old costumes from school plays, boxes of old library books, and one or two new stand up dollys. Just as Naimah was rolling Liz out from backstage on one of the dollys, Eddie came across some co-axles that would fit the outputs in back of his stereo.

"Turn on the radio," yelled Liz. Eddie turned the radio on and got a loud crackling sound instead of music, soon followed by a loud POP! And then smoke.

"Man!" Eddie sounded exasperated. "Just blew a fuse!"

"You don't have it hooked up right," offered Anthony. "Here," he said, "let me take a look." While the two boys fumbled with the cables and sound system, Naimah and Tayesha walked around the gym pointing out the best way to decorate for the dance while Liz sat center stage shouting out suggestions.

"Let's loop crepe paper along the walls and see if we can get Mr. King to help us string it into a pyramid from the center of the ceiling," suggested Liz.

"Yeah," agreed Tayesha. "We'll need a ladder. And for that Mr. King is the answer."

"And let's add atmosphere with some of those flashing lights Sandy used at her birthday party last year," Naimah offered.

"That's a great idea, Naimah," said Liz excitedly, getting into the party mood. "Sandy's lights can be set to blink to the beat of the music. That will be so cool."

"Yeah," said Tayesha, "just think how cool it would be to have those lights bumping to *rap* music." Liz groaned.

"Do you have to remind me?" she moaned. The thought of having nothing to dance to except heavy metal had suddenly brought her down.

"Not to worry," Naimah tried to brighten the moment. "We still have a little over a week left. Anything can happen—"

"A minor miracle would work," Liz sighed.

"Keep your chin up, Liz," Naimah consoled her friend. "I haven't given up on the import booth. Not yet anyway. I think we should take Eddie's advice and try wearing some of the garments and some of the jewelry to school. It just might help boost sales."

"Sounds good to me," said Tayesha. "I've had my eye set on one of those beautiful lappas. I think Eddie was right," she said primping her Afro. "One of those African dresses *would* go nicely with my hair."

"Go for it, girlfriend," smiled Liz.

"We'll all wear something from the booth to school tomorrow. Who knows? We might inspire somebody," speculated Naimah.

All of a sudden static from Eddie's radio traveled over the school's P.A. system. As quickly as they'd heard it, it went dead again.

"Be with you ladies in just a minute," promised Eddie, looking up from behind the stereo equipment.

"I think you're right, Naimah," said Liz. "It's a shot in the dark but who knows. Maybe we can get enough things sold between now and next week to get the money to hire a band."

"Maybe you could still get one of the bands

from the auditions to play for us," said Tayesha hopefully.

"I'm sure I could if we could only raise the money. That would only be half the battle. And speaking of auditions," Liz reminded herself, "I've got to get some ice on this ankle as soon as I get home. Half of my act is the dancing."

"At least you got your voice back," Naimah offered encouragement.

"But how am I supposed to get on stage?" whined Liz. "And once I get on stage, how am I supposed to dance?"

"Tell you what," offered Tayesha, "you work on getting that ankle of yours in shape and Naimah and I will put our heads together and see if we can't come up with a way to get you up on stage."

"Have you decided on a song yet?" Naimah asked, trying to get Liz's thoughts back on the right track.

"I'm still stuck between SWV and Mary J. Blige. They'll let me use background vocals from the CD and sing my own lead on which ever song I choose."

"I like SWV better," admitted Tayesha.

"And I like Mary J. Blige," said Naimah.

"Well, I like them both," said Liz. "And the closer it gets to next week the harder it is to decide." Suddenly the gymnasium was filled with the harsh, loud sound of static popping over electrical wires. Then, just as unexpectedly, the music of radio station V93 pushed through the feedback.

"You are so fine, so fine
So fine you blow my mind,
With the things you do.
She is not fine, not fine, not fine
She's not so fine. . ."

"The things you do for me, and I am, I'm so into you. . ." Liz joined in with SWV. She hopped up on her one good foot, hobbled over to the microphone, and sang in perfect harmony with the radio music while Eddie, Naimah, Anthony, and Tayesha bumped and jammed to the rhythms of their talented friend.

◆ CHAPTER THIRTEEN ◆

By five o'clock Liz, Naimah, Eddie, and Tayesha were making their way down the steps of the school. Anthony had left as soon as the sound system had been checked out. He'd had papers to deliver. And now as they approached the sidewalk in front of DuSable, Tayesha headed in the opposite direction of her friends who were headed home towards Mary Street.

Tayesha waved good-bye to her friends and began slowly walking to the corner in front of the junior high school. The day had started out sunny and warm, but as Tayesha turned the corner for her grandmother's house the sky suddenly became cloudy and a cool brisk wind began to pick up.

Tayesha thought she felt a drop of rain on her cheek. She felt inside her bookbag for her cap. When she didn't find it she convinced herself that she had better walk faster if she didn't want to get caught in a downpour. She was making good time when suddenly she looked up and in the distance saw that the basketball court was empty. A load seemed to be lifted off her chest. Her feet suddenly felt as light as wings. In no time at all Tayesha found herself crossing the alley that would put her on the sidewalk next to the tall cyclone fence surrounding the court. From there it was only a block to her grandmother's house.

Just as Tayesha was about to step off the curb she felt something cold smash into her face. It landed on her eye and slid down her chin and down across the front of her jacket.

"BULL'S EYE!" she heard someone shout. Tayesha wiped her eye and looked down at her jacket where she saw the remains of a mound of chocolate-chip ice cream oozing down the front of her jacket and pants. She wanted to cry. But the person who had thrown the ice cream bomb at her didn't plan on giving her a chance to cry.

"Hey oreo," laughed a familiar voice from behind her. Tayesha whirled around to find one of her basketball court tormentors.

"My. . ." stuttered Tayesha, trying desperately to keep the tears in her throat from spilling out of her eyes.

"My. . ." mimicked another of one of the hecklers, jumping from the alley onto the sidewalk.

"Yo! Check it out, man," laughed the third boy, dangling an empty sugar cone behind Tayesha's head. "Yo, man look! Oreo's got a new hair do. She almost looks like a black person now. Almost."

All three boys began laughing at Tayesha. Tayesha wanted to run to her grandmother's house as fast as she could. But instead she stood there swallowing hard, trying to fight back the tears. Suddenly all she could think about was Anthony. That night a couple of weeks ago on her porch steps, and what he'd said to her:

"The next time you walk past that basketball court, WALK! Don't run. And you tell those jerks that your name ain't oreo. . . ."

Tayesha wiped the rest of the ice cream from her eye. The three jerks were still laughing and the one who'd thrown the ice cream was galloping around Tayesha in a tight circle. He was pointing the empty cone at her. They were all shouting.

"My name is not oreo!" Tayesha yelled.

Loud enough so that she even startled herself. And to her surprise, the three hecklers suddenly became quiet. The boy with the empty cone dropped it. The cone went smashing to the sidewalk.

"My name is Tayesha!" she yelled again as though the three boys had been too far away the first time to hear her shout. "And if you want to talk to me, you call me by my real name." The three hecklers had been caught off guard. The one standing behind Tayesha began to back quietly away. Tayesha spun around.

"What's *your* name?" Tayesha asked him.

Reluctantly, the boy admitted, "I'm Bubba." Tayesha spun around again, now facing the two remaining troublemakers.

"I'm Chris," responded the boy who had thrown the scoop of ice cream.

"I'm Miles," admitted the last culprit.

"And I'm Tayesha," Tayesha reminded them. "I'm not oreo, Bubba. Or oreo cookie, Chris. Or all-mixed-up, Miles. I'm just Tayesha. And I'm as much a black person as you. At least I know that black people come in different shades. So I wish you'd call me Tayesha the next time you want to talk to me."

"Yeah. Yeah. Yeah," the three boys murmured and then just walked away. After they reached the corner Tayesha wiped her eye again and took a deep breath. As she walked the last block past the court, all Tayesha could think about was Anthony. She couldn't wait to see him tomorrow at school.

When she reached her grandmother's lawn Tayesha saw her father's buick parked out front. She didn't stop on the front porch this time. This time she ran right into the vestibule. Rang the bell. And smiled at the beautiful, honey-colored reflection of herself in her grandmother's mirror.

◆ CHAPTER FOURTEEN ◆

It was Monday morning in the Delaney house and only four days before the school dance. Eddie had just finished dressing for school. He wore the African garment he'd selected from the NEATE import booth. With only a few days left to raise money for the rap band, Eddie was really banking on people buying more items based upon how good they looked on him, Anthony, Tayesha, Naimah, and Liz.

Eddie stood transfixed in front of his bedroom mirror. This strategy had to work. He was dressed in an agbada, a four-piece traditional African suit with dashiki, pants, a poncho-like over vest, and a matching kofia. The suit was black embossed silk embroidered with gold piping. Eddie ran his hand down the gold piping of his vest and straightened the crease in his pants.

He thought he looked handsome. As he stood there with his chin uplifted and his shoulders pressed back into attention like a soldier his father knocked on the door.

"Hi, Dad," said Eddie a little embarrassed.

"Good morning, son," smiled Mr. Delaney from behind a cup of steaming coffee. For a moment they were both silent.

"Well?" said Eddie breaking the ice. "How do I look?"

"You look fine, son," smiled Mr. Delaney setting his coffee mug on Eddie's bureau. "You look like a prince. But something's missing," said his father reaching into his back pocket and unfolding a long royal blue, black and gold embroidered Kente strip. Eddie's eyes grew wide with disbelief. He couldn't believe his father was letting him wear his gold-dust Kente. Mr. Delaney draped the Kente strip around Eddie's neck.

"Now you really look like a prince," Eddie's father beamed at him. "Your mother told me that you're the one who came up with the idea of having your friends wear clothes from the import booth."

"Your gold-dust Kente, Dad," Eddie whispered at his image in the mirror.

"That gold dust was given to me when I served as guest ambassador to Ghana before you were born. Traditionally," explained Eddie's father, "only members of royalty wore Kente cloth."

"I promise I'll take good care of it, Dad," said Eddie studying the colorful geometrical designs with his fingertips.

"I hope you do take good care of it, son," said Mr. Delaney, "because it doesn't belong to me anymore. It belongs to you." Eddie turned from the mirror and faced his father. He reached out to shake his father's hand but quickly decided against it. Instead, Eddie gave his old man a hug.

By lunch time the import booth was mass hysteria.

"And these are cowry shells," explained Liz flashing the cowry shell bracelet she wore on her wrist to a group of girls gathered at the booth. "Cowry shells bring good luck. We also have cowry shell necklaces and earrings."

While Liz's audience tried on jewelry, Tayesha busied herself collecting payments from teachers who'd purchased gifts on Eddie's easy payment plan. And Eddie collected payments from all the girls like Camilla whom he'd sold items to on lay-away.

"Listen, Camilla," said Eddie bagging up her purchase. "All this talk about African imports and stuff was really my way of leading up to asking if you'd go to the dance with me on Friday night."

"Well, I don't know, Eddie," teased Camilla. "What about all the other girls who bought things from you on time?"

"All the others were pay-as-you-go," Eddie grinned, "but with you? Well, with you I was always hoping to establish a major account."

"Oh, Eddie," Camilla blushed.

"Yo, Anthony!" yelled Casey Collins heading for the booth. Casey had a paper route just like Anthony and sometimes they delivered papers together. "Man! I really like that dashiki you're wearing," admired Casey. "Got another one like it?"

"Sorry, Man!" said Anthony. "This is the last of the dashikis like this one. And Tayesha likes it on me so much that *I've* decided to buy it myself." Anthony dug deep inside his pocket and pulled out his money. He counted out twenty-two dollars and handed it to Naimah who was managing the cash box.

"Big spender," smiled Naimah.

"Yup, and it's all for a good cause," Anthony

winked. By the end of the lunch hour Naimah counted three hundred dollars, not including the twenty-five dollars they'd raised a week ago on their first dry run at selling imports.

"Aaah!" screamed Liz. "Can you believe this, girlfriend? We are going to be thumpin' and bumpin' and jammin' to the beat of rap come Friday night."

"With only four days left, what kind of band can we get?" Anthony asked doubtfully.

"The Rap Meisters!" drooled Liz.

"Oh, yeah?" Eddie jumped in. "Those were the guys who wore the Kente cloth baseball caps at the V93 auditions."

"Right," laughed Tayesha and Naimah.

"Right," smiled Liz. "The Rap Meisters. They aren't booked. They say if we have the money, they're available. With the lead singer who is *so-o-o* fine!"

◆ CHAPTER FIFTEEN ◆

Friday night Liz stood in her bedroom mirror dressed in a pair of white baggies with brilliant colors splashed all over them and a royal blue Cross Colours jacket. Liz stuck a small single hoop earring in her right ear, laid on a black Chicago Bulls cap and was ready to party, if not dance.

When she reached the DuSable gym the pulsating sound of the Rap Meisters greeted her. Inside, two bands were set up in a face off. One heavy metal. The other one rap. Overhead, Sandy's lights blinked to the rhythm of rap. Liz entered the gym and shuffled across the floor to the beat of the loud music.

The place was jam packed. Liz wasted no time in looking for her posse. As she pushed through the crowd both teachers and students showered her with well wishes for tomorrow night's talent contest. Someone pulled on her jacket. She turned around to find Le standing behind her in the crowd. Together they helped pull each other out of the knotted circle.

"My brother was really impressed with you," Le began, shouting over the music. "You know so much about music."

"Thanks," said Liz, "but not as much as you and your brother do," she returned the compliment. They stood there talking and grooving to the music.

Le tapped Liz on the shoulder, "You want to dance?" he asked. They both looked down at Liz's ankle and laughed. At that moment Pete Russell was sliding past the pair trying to do the robot to heavy metal music.

"Ugh!" Liz groaned. "Let's show butthead how to 'get down.' "

"But—what about your ankle?" Le stammered.

Liz grabbed Le's hand. "My condition may be critical," she smiled, "but I'm not dead. Not yet anyway."

In another corner of the room Eddie was busy trying to rap to Camilla.

"Hey," he said. "You really look good in that head wrap."

Camilla smiled and said, "Eddie, I'll bet you'd say so even if you didn't think so."

"And I'll bet you'd think so even if I didn't say so," Eddie smiled back at her. A slow ballad hit the airwaves and Eddie took Camilla by the hand. "Come on, Camilla," he said. "Let's dance."

Tayesha and Anthony were already out on the dance floor, their arms tied loosely around each other. Tayesha's honey-colored face looked almost bronze under the flashing gymnasium lights. Her Afro hairstyle framed her face in a soft crown.

"I like your hair," said Anthony, "before and after," he teased Tayesha.

"Thanks," said Tayesha with a shy smile. And then, as an after thought, she said, "I like *your* hair, too."

"And your skin," Anthony went on.

"And your eyes," said Tayesha smiling bashfully.

"And my eyes," said Anthony. And then the young couple laughed at each other.

"Thanks for being my friend," Tayesha whispered in Anthony's ear. And then they fell silent and just danced to the music:

> *"And if I ever fall in love again,*
> *I will be sure that the lady is my friend. . ."*

◆ CHAPTER SIXTEEN ◆

The crowd at the Palladium was flowing in and around the concert hall like ants working in an ant colony. Inside the club, the house lights were on, but spotlights searched and scanned over the audience as though the talent show had already begun.

While Liz's mother and father escorted her backstage, Sandy, Angie, Naimah, Eddie, Anthony, and Tayesha managed to find floor seats.

"This is exciting," said Sandy surveying the crowd. "There are more people here than at the last competition Liz was in."

"There are definitely more girls here," Eddie quickly confirmed shouting over the noise of the crowd. "I'll bet there are at least three girls here for every boy."

"Well, gee I don't know, Eddie," Naimah

teased her friend. "Wouldn't it depend on what the boy looks like?"

"Like me," Eddie shot back. "The boy looks like me."

"That's what I thought," said Naimah cracking up. Eddie gave her a friendly shove.

"Hey, look!" Tayesha pointed toward center stage. "That's Ron Cornelius from Dance Train."

"It sure looks like him," said Sandy standing to get a better look.

"It is him," confirmed Anthony pointing now himself. "And that's Roz Carter, the traveling D.J., with him."

"And now! . . . " a voice rang out from center stage, "the V93 star talent search for this city's next shining star. . . . Tonight's live show is being broadcast over the radio waves of station V93." Suddenly the audience began to whistle fiercely in anticipation of the opening act. And the slender, multi-colored-neon wand lights sold by vendors before the opening of the show, were now being used by the audience to penetrate the darkness of the club.

"And now!" the radio voice rang out, "help me give a large round of applause to the Rap Meisters, representing Carver High School!" The stage lights flashed on and off and the Carver High school contingency laid out a thick welcome mat for their own. There were cameras flashing everywhere. And the audience screamed so loudly that the music from the soundstage was at times barely even audible.

The Rap Meisters were freshmen from Carver High School. They did a medley of rap songs from the group Da Youngsta's, and got a standing ovation on a Saturday morning groove called "Cartoon."

The next act was from Marshall High, a Caribbean-Calypso soul band that highlighted a Shabba Ranks sound. The whole auditorium reverberated to the heartbeat of the drums.

Following it was a singles act from Tennyson Junior High School. A seventh grader from the city's South Side drew fresh applause with her Monie Love Review, and the hit single, "Monie In The Middle."

Then the Children of Soul choir from Roosevelt High sang three gospel jumpers that brought the audience to its feet. The competition was stiff.

By intermission, Liz had gathered quite a support group herself. Eddie had seen Ms. Lewis, the DuSable music teacher, at the concession stand. The DuSable chorus members and half the school band were there. And even Le had fought the push of the crowd to come over and find a seat sitting with Eddie, Tayesha, Anthony, and Naimah.

When the house lights began to dim again, the Butler family and friends didn't have to wait much longer to cheer the talent they had come to hear. In the midst of shouts and shrieking whistles, above the roar of the crowd the radio voice announced: "And now, ladies and gentlemen! For the final half of our show, please join me in welcoming an especially talented eighth grader from the city's West Side, DuSable Junior High School's Ms. Liz Butler singing SWV's hit single, 'I'm So Into You!'"

Thump, bump! Thump, bump! . . . The music to Liz's popular Sister's With Voices song opened up to a wild round of applause. The audience went crazy when Liz, dressed in a red leather jump suit, flashing her million dollar smile and waving at the audience like a true star, was rolled onto the stage by two stage hands on a brightly painted silver metallic dolly, right up to the microphone, in a barrage of flashing cameras, screams, whistles, and roving spotlights that criss-crossed her path. At the microphone, Liz danced in place and pumped to the pulsating stage music.

"Boy, there you go
You're telling me, that you love me.
But boy you know that you belong
to another girl who loves you.
You are so fine, so fine,
So fine you blow my mind
With the things you do.
She sees she's not fine
She's not fine. . .
Things you do for me but I am—
I'm so into you,
I don't know what I'm gonna do.
You know you got me so confused.
I'm so confused—
I don't know what I'm gonna do. . ."

By the time Liz had finished her performance the whole audience was perspiring. People who didn't even know her were giving each other high fives. That's how good she was. She was the only act called back for an encore.

By the time the last act had performed Mr. and Ms. Butler and their entourage had worked their way backstage. There they found a dozen long-stemmed red roses sitting in Liz's dressing room.

"These are beautiful!" exclaimed Ms. Butler. "And so were you, honey," she smiled, hugging her daughter.

"Yes, they are beautiful," agreed Mr. Butler frowning. "*Who* are they from?"

"Oh, Daddy!" declared Liz, "I don't even know," she said opening the card that came with the flowers. "Oh, Daddy!" she smiled broadly this time giving both her parents a huge bear hug. "They're from you and Mama."

"You were great, Liz!" Naimah jumped in.

"Yeah, you really were good this time, ugly," teased Eddie.

"Knocked them dead," smiled Tayesha.

"Yeah," agreed Anthony.

"You out did yourself this time, Sis," said Sandy leaning over to give her younger sister a kiss.

"I bet you win the prize," said a small voice from in between Mr. Butler's tall legs. It was little Angie. Liz picked her little sister up and gave her a hug.

"I hope so, Angie," reflected Liz. "This prize means more to me than any prize I've ever won." Then suddenly she noticed Le standing behind the small crowd of family and friends.

"Le!" Liz said surprised. "What are you doing here?"

Le smiled. "I guess you might say I was hungry for a little soul music," he said.

"Well, I guess you must've gotten yourself a bellyful tonight," teased Mr. Butler which made everybody laugh. Just then one of the program sponsors raced back into the dressing room where Liz had gathered with her family and friends.

"Liz!" she said almost out of breath. "Liz Butler! They need you back on stage," she was practically shouting. "Go stand in the wings! I think you may have won first place!"

Liz stood on stage basking in the light and the cheers of the huge Palladium crowd. As she waved and blew kisses she was close to tears.

By the time she and her small entourage made it backstage to collect her belongings, a small crowd had gathered. Congratulations were flying everywhere.

"Congratulations, girlfriend," smiled Naimah hugging her best friend. "I love you, Liz. I knew you could do it."

Wiping tears from her eyes, Liz answered, "If you think you love me now, girlfriend, just wait until you hear the announcement I'm about to make." And then Liz's father helped her climb up on a dressing room chair. All of her best friends were there. Her family, Ms. Lewis, and even some kids from DuSable.

"Listen, everybody," Liz shouted over the clamoring voices. "I have an announcement to make. As the crowd grew silent, Liz began to explain. "As I said a few moments ago on stage, I'm really thrilled to win the grand prize for the V93 contest. I'm especially happy because I almost didn't make it here tonight to compete. If it weren't for the support of all of you, none of this would've happened for me," Liz looked at all the faces packed in the door and crowded together in the tiny room.

"So tonight I'd like to show my appreciation." Liz's eyes searched the crowd until she found Le's face. "I have a couple of new friends who are facing the real possibility of becoming homeless in the next few days, that is, if someone doesn't step up to save the shelter they live in. The other people living in the shelter don't know me. But I promise I won't let that stop me from doing the right thing. A couple of weeks ago, someone mentioned that it would take a miracle to raise the money needed to save the shelter, and keep the people living there from becoming homeless." Liz looked down at her father and took the piece of paper that he held up to her from his hand. She held up a check for $2,500, her share of the prize money from tonight's V93 talent contest.

"I hope this check will help keep the Queen Street shelter open. I don't know that it's what the people who live there have been hoping for. But my wish is that it will help keep them all off the street."

There was a huge round of applause, almost as deafening as the sound that had filled the auditorium earlier with the announcement of the grand prize winner. In the back of the crowd stood Le smiling and waving vigorously at Liz. His brother Tan, who had arrived late, stood next to him waving and mouthing the words: "Congratulations, soul sister!" Liz winked at her two new friends, and smiled her million dollar star smile at both of them.

About the Author

Debbi Chocolate is a writer, storyteller and educator. She received a bachelor's degree from Spelman College in Atlanta, Georgia and a master's degree from Brown University in Providence, Rode Island. She has worked as an editor, a high school English teacher, and her written work has appeared in a number of national magazines.

Ms. Chocolate is the author of several picture books. They include *Kwanzaa*, published by Children's Press and *My First Kwanzaa Book*, published by Scholastic, Inc. *Elizabeth's Wish* is her second published novel for older readers.

MEET

NAIMAH

Naimah is a proud, self-assured thirteen year old. A born leader, she enjoys coming up with answers to difficult situations. Everyone says she looks just like her mother, who is a member of city council. Naimah loves the comparison. Naimah's mother has remarried and Naimah is fond of her step-dad. But her little brother Rodney, however, is another story. To her, he is the "human-pest."

ELIZABETH

Liz just knows she is going to be *the* next pop superstar. She can sing and has won a number of talent shows, but she tends to overdo it a bit. Liz wears leather suits and other flashy garb her father buys for her. One week, her hair is long and flowing. The next week it is in braids. She is always searching for a new style. But, she is a "singer," isn't she?

ANTHONY

TAYESHA

EDDIE

Anthony is very bright and studious. He is smaller than other kids his age, and sometimes that annoys him. Anthony's mother is a single parent and he has never seen his father. He feels that he is the man of the house and must take care of his mother. She is, however, very capable of taking care of herself and Anthony. Anthony works hard at everything he does and wants to be a lawyer like Eddie's father.

Tayesha's father is African American and her mother is German. Her parents met when her father, an army veteran, was stationed in Germany. Tayesha is quite sensitive about her interracial background. She has always been aware of the stares her family receives wherever they go. Quick to stand up for the underdog, Tayesha doesn't understand why some people can be so mean and hateful.

Eddie's given name is Martin Edward Delaney, but everyone calls him Eddie. He prefers it that way. Eddie's father named him after Dr. Martin Luther King, Jr. and never lets him forget it. "You've got to have drive and determination, Eddie, if you want to succeed. You can't be lazy." That's Eddie's father. "Sure, Dad," Eddie is apt to respond. Eddie loves sports, although he is not really good at any one of them.

Tell Us What You Think About NEATE™!

Name _____

Address _____

City _____ State ____ Zip _____

Date of Birth _____

1. Who is your favorite NEATE™ character? _____

2. What kind of story would you like to see NEATE™ take on?
    (a) mystery (b) adventure (c) romance (d) other _____

3. How did you get your first copy of NEATE™?
    (a) parent (b) gift (c) own purchase (d) other _____

4. Are you looking forward to the next title in the NEATE™ series?
    (a) yes (b) no _____
        If no, why? _____
_____
_____

5. Is there anything else you'd like to add? _____
_____
_____
_____
_____

Send your reply to
Editor: NEATE™
    c/o Just Us Books, Inc.
       356 Glenwood Avenue
       East Orange, NJ 07017

OTHER TITLES FROM JUST US BOOKS

AFRO-BETS® Book of Black Heroes From A to Z
by Wade Hudson and Valerie Wilson Wesley

Book of Black Heroes Vol 2:
Great Women in the Struggle ed. by Toyomi Igus

Bright Eyes, Brown Skin by Cheryl Willis Hudson
and Bernette Ford, illustrated by George Ford

Jamal's Busy Day by Wade Hudson, illustrated by
George Ford

When I Was Little by Toyomi Igus, illustrated by
Higgins Bond

Also . . .

AFRO-BETS® A B C Book by Cheryl Willis Hudson

AFRO-BETS® 1 2 3 Book by Cheryl Willis Hudson

AFRO-BETS® Book of Colors by Margery W. Brown

AFRO-BETS® Book of Shapes by Margery W. Brown

AFRO-BETS® First Book About Africa by Veronica Freeman Ellis,
illustrated by George Ford

AFRO-BETS® Activity and Coloring Book by Dwayne Ferguson

AFRO-BETS® Kids: I'm Gonna Be! by Wade Hudson,
illustrated by Culverson Blair

Land of the Four Winds by Veronica Freeman Ellis,
illustrated by Sylvia Walker

Please visit our website for current publications www.justusbooks.com